Rabbit and Hare Divide an Apple

A Viking Math Easy-to-Read

by Harriet Ziefert

illustrated by Emily Bolam

VIKING

VIKING
Published by the Penguin Group
Penguin Books USA Inc., 375 Hudson Street, New York, New York 10014, U.S.A.
Penguin Books Ltd, 27 Wrights Lane, London W8 5TZ, England
Penguin Books Australia Ltd, Ringwood, Victoria, Australia
Penguin Books Canada Ltd, 10 Alcorn Avenue, Toronto, Ontario, Canada M4V 3B2
Penguin Books (N.Z.) Ltd, 182–190 Wairau Road, Auckland 10, New Zealand

Penguin Books Ltd, Registered Offices: Harmondsworth, Middlesex, England

First published in 1998 by Viking, a member of Penguin Putnam Inc.
Published simultaneously in Puffin Books

1 3 5 7 9 10 8 6 4 2

LIBRARY OF CONGRESS CATALOGING-IN-PUBLICATION DATA
Ziefert, Harriet.
Rabbit and Hare divide an apple / by Harriet Ziefert ; illustrated
by Emily Bolam.
p. cm. — (A Viking math easy-to-read. Level 1)
Summary: Because both Rabbit and Hare insist on having the larger
piece of mushroom, they lose the whole thing to a sly raccoon but
learn an important lesson in the process.
ISBN 0-670-87790-5 (hc). — ISBN 0-14-038820-6 (pbk.)
[1. Fractions—Fiction. 2. Division—Fiction. 3. Sharing—Fiction.]
I. Bolam, Emily, ill. II. Title. III. Series.
PZ7.Z487Rab 1998 [E]—dc21 97-25781 CIP AC

Printed in U.S.A.
Set in Bookman

Reading level 1.7

Rabbit and Hare Divide an Apple

Rabbit and Hare loved to eat.
One day they found
a big mushroom.

Rabbit said, "We can break it in half. Then each of us can eat one piece."

Rabbit broke the mushroom.
But not in half!

One piece was a little bigger
than the other.

Hare grabbed the bigger piece.
"This one is mine!" he said.

"No, it isn't!" said Rabbit.
And he grabbed it back.

Just then Mr. Raccoon walked by.
"What is the matter?" he asked.

Rabbit said, "We have two pieces
of mushroom. One piece is bigger
than the other."

"And I want the bigger piece!"
said Hare.

"I know what to do," said Mr. Raccoon.
"I'll take a bite from the bigger piece.
I'll make them equal—both the same."

Mr. Raccoon took a bite and…

he ate the whole piece!

"Now we have only one piece
of mushroom," cried Hare.

"I know what to do," said Mr. Raccoon.
"I'll bite this piece in half.
   Then you'll have two pieces."

Mr. Raccoon took a bite and...

ate the whole thing up!

Rabbit and Hare cried,
"It's all gone!
All gone!"

Mr. Raccoon left quickly—
very quickly.

"Now what do we do?"
asked Hare.

"Let's find something else
to eat," said Rabbit.

They found an apple—
big and round.

Hare tried to divide
the apple in half.

But one piece was much
bigger than the other.

Rabbit grabbed the bigger piece.
"This one is mine!" he said.

"Oh no it isn't!" said Hare.

And he grabbed it back!

"I'll help you," Mr. Raccoon said.
"I'll divide the bigger piece in half.

Then we'll have three pieces—
all equal. One for each of us."

"Oh no you won't!"
said Rabbit.

"We can divide our
own apple!" said Hare.

"First we'll split the big part.
And then we'll split the
small piece."

And they did!

How many ways can you divide an apple?
What else can you divide in half?
A piece of paper? A cup of water?
Is it hard or easy to divide things equally?